The SockKids™
Say NO To Bullying

By Michael John Sullivan
and Shelley Larkin

Illustrations by
Alexandra Gold

ISBN 9780991154166

LCCN 2016906876

The SockKids books are available to purchase for
schools, libraries, organizations, and individuals.

R ing! Ringgg! Riiinnnnggggg! The human's alarm clock shook the snoozing SockKids from their sleepy slumber. Rainbow, the loving mother sock, nudged her always adventurous son, Sudsy. "Sweetie, it's time to wake up. Your human needs you today. Do you know why?"

Sudsy stretched his green and orange

fabric and inflated like a balloon when it fills with helium. This caused his baby sister, Sunni, to giggle. He let out a long, loooonnnng yawn. He asked in a weak voice, "Why, Mom, does my human need me?"

Rainbow smiled, her many colors brightening with love. "Because even humans need love and we are here to share it with them."

She lifted Sudsy up. "Do you need a wash?"

Sudsy shook his head. "No. I had one last night. Can't you tell?" He lifted his arm.

Rainbow leaned in and backed away. "My, you could certainly use a quick soaping."

Before Rainbow could finish her thought, Sudsy jumped out of the drawer,

spread his arms like a super hero, and floated down to the carpet.

Sudsy gave a big wave to Sunni and his mother before rolling away down the hallway. He stopped rolling near his human's bed. "Ethan, where are you?" he called out.

Sudsy grew excited when his human entered the room and picked him up. Ethan placed Sudsy on his right foot. Much to his surprise, his shy brother, Wooly, was on Ethan's other leg.

"Why are you here?" Sudsy asked in a curious tone.

Wooly shrugged. "I was on his foot when he was reading a book. He hasn't taken me off since then."

"That's strange," said Sudsy. "He'll take you off soon because Ethan never takes you to school."

"You're probably right," agreed Wooly.

Sudsy and Wooly waited for Ethan to make the sock change. However, much to the SockKids' surprise, Ethan wore them both to school.

Ethan arrived at school to discover that the new girl, Olivia, was sitting alone.

Olivia was reading the same book he was! Ethan was excited and decided to say hello until a group of tough boys started laughing as he approached her. They waved their hands to tell Ethan to stop.

Ethan did stop, not sure what to do as more boys and girls gathered to watch

him. "What are you doing?" asked a bigger boy. "Are you going to read with her?"

Ethan could hear the group of boys and girls laugh louder. His stomach rumbled and he looked down at the floor, unsure what to do. "Are you okay?" asked the girl.

Ethan couldn't answer and instead walked away.

"Where are you going?" shouted the bigger boy.

"Are you going to the library?" another boy asked. He laughed.

Ethan walked into the hallway, outside the lunch area. He took a deep breath.

"Are you sick?" asked the girl with the book, peeking her head out.

Ethan didn't say anything to the girl. She left and Ethan slowly walked back into the lunch room. He had been excited to eat lunch and had planned to sit at the same table with the tough boys. But he was embarrassed. "No one will sit with me at lunch now," he thought to himself. He sat alone at a desk.

He saw Olivia sitting by herself at

the far end of the room, reading that same book. His heart raced at the possibility of talking about it with her. He so desperately wanted to until the tough boys arrived and one slapped him on his back. "Good to see you are with us now," one boy said with a big laugh. He grabbed Ethan's book, the one he wanted to show Olivia, tore

several pages out of it, and tossed it into the garbage can. "You're not going to need this."

Ethan looked at the garbage can. He stared for several seconds while the boys continued to mock Olivia.

Sudsy reached over and tapped Wooly. "That's so sad."

"I wish we could help," Wooly said.

"Maybe we can. Let's put our heads together and come up with a plan," Sudsy replied.

Stretch and Wooly began tickling Ethan's feet. Ethan sat down on the floor, pulling his sneakers and socks off to see what was tickling him. Behind his back, Stretch and Wooly rolled off toward the garbage can.

"Yeah, we thought you were with her," another boy said, distracting

Ethan from his runaway socks. "She's a nerd. Nerds read books. We don't hang around nerds." The tough boy pointed at Olivia, sitting quietly, not bothering anyone, reading her book.

Ethan felt uncomfortable and excused himself. "I need to go to the bathroom," he said, hesitating.

"Where's your socks?" mocked one boy, pointing at Ethan's feet.

Ethan looked around for Wooly and Stretch. They were nowhere to be seen.

"Go ahead," said another tough boy. "But you may lose that seat next to us."

"And you'll have to pay us to get it back," added another boy. "Do you have lunch money today? We're going to need more money."

Ethan didn't answer. He looked back

for a quick second to see if the tough boys were watching. They were too busy, laughing and picking on another boy. As he walked past Olivia, she looked up and smiled. "Hi," she said.

Ethan froze. "Who? Me?"

"Yes, you. Who do you think I was talking to?" Her smile grew.

"Hi. I see you are reading the same book as me. Do you like it?" Ethan asked.

"I do. This story is wonderful. I love to read. Where is your book? I thought you had it with you." She looked down at his feet. "What happened to your socks?"

Ethan looked away, embarrassed over what had happened.

"What's wrong?" Olivia asked.

"Those boys took my book and threw it in the garbage," Ethan replied.

"They did what?" Olivia got up. "The garbage can over there?"

"Yes," Ethan said. "But don't go over there."

The boys surrounded the garbage can, laughing and picking on the same boy, kicking his bag around like

a soccer ball along the floor. Olivia walked into the middle of the group and looked into the garbage can. To her surprise, Sudsy was holding the book and Wooly offered her the torn pages.

She accepted the book and pages and grabbed Sudsy and Wooly. They sat on her shoulders as Olivia picked up

the school bag and gave it back to the boy. Then she started to walk through the crowd.

"Hey, what are you doing?" one of them demanded.

"She's getting my book," said Ethan, stepping in. "Let's go, Olivia."

The boys mocked them both as they walked back to the table where Olivia had been sitting. "I think these are yours," she said with a big smile, handing Sudsy and Wooly back to him.

Ethan smiled. "They are the best sock buddies."

Olivia and Ethan sat down after he put Sudsy and Wooly back on his feet. He noticed Olivia also had a sketch book. "Do you draw, too?"

Olivia nodded. "Yes! Do you want to see some of my drawings?"

"Oh, do I," said Ethan with a rush of enthusiasm. He sat down next to her.

Olivia pulled out several illustrations, many of them of cats and dogs. "I have a cat. Her name is Seashell. She's the sweetest cat. When I'm at school, I miss her. I think she misses me too. She cries when I leave. Seashell had her own cat friends in our old neighborhood. I think she misses them."

"I'm sorry your cat is sad," Ethan said, sitting down next to her. "I know that must be difficult."

"Leaving my friends behind was tough too," Olivia said. "I miss my friends back home."

"You have me as a friend," Ethan said with a smile.

"Thank you," Olivia said with a big smile. "What do you like to do?"

Ethan moved closer. "I like to play baseball and I like to spend time with my friends."

"What do you do with your friends?" Olivia asked.

"We talk about how we can help others in our neighborhood. We raise

money to help the homeless so they can eat a good meal. We try to help people who are in need."

"That sounds wonderful," Olivia said.

"Maybe you would be interested in joining us?" Ethan asked. "We're always looking for more friends to help us."

Olivia smiled again. "I would love to help out."

Ethan stood and stared ahead at the tough boys watching him. "I'm going to talk to my friends and tell them you want to help us. I'll ask them when we walk home from school. We see each other almost every day."

"Thank you!" said Olivia.

"See you!" Ethan said as he waved goodbye.

After school, Ethan spoke to his friends. "Who is this girl?" asked Joey.

"Her name is Olivia. She's kind and nice and wants to help us out in the neighborhood," Ethan said.

"I know her," Sarah added. "She rocks! And she loves to read."

Ethan stopped walking and the others

did as well. "I like to read, too," he said. "Those boys made fun of Olivia because she was reading. They were mean. They called her names."

"Those boys were wrong. Next time, tell a teacher what is happening. If you enjoy reading, then you should read. I read as much as I can," Sarah said.

"Me too," Joey said, holding his hand up for a high five.

They all slapped hands together.

Sudsy looked at his brother, who looked sad. "What's wrong, Wooly?"

"Some of the socks in the bottom drawer called me names and they made fun of me because I like to read," said Wooly. "They laughed at me." Wooly looked down at the floor. "Now I understand how Ethan felt when those boys threw his book in the trash can. It made me feel good to help Ethan."

Wooly hesitated. "Is there something wrong with me because I like to read more than I like to play sports?" he asked.

Sudsy stretched his fabric to pat his brother. "No. There isn't anything wrong with you just because you are different from others or have different interests. Every sock is different. We have different colors. We're made of different fabric. We have different shapes and sizes. We even have different soap issues." Sudsy lifted his arm and smelled it.

Wooly looked up and laughed.

Sudsy winked. "I'm always here for

you, little brother. If someone bullies you, let's tell Mom and Dad."

Their human friends gathered together to have a discussion. "I vote her in," Sarah said.

"I do, too," Wooly yelled.

"Me, too," Sudsy said, trying to catch the humans' attention. "Can they hear us?"

"I think so!" said Wooly.

Joey looked at Ethan and Sarah. "Yes, I vote her in too. I also didn't know you liked to read, Ethan. We have to talk more about what you do read."

"We will," Ethan said. "Can Olivia join us on the walk home tomorrow from school?"

"Yes," they shouted in unison.

Oh, what a big day it was for Ethan and his friends. They were eager to have Olivia help them with their new experiences and challenges. They couldn't wait for the school bell to ring the next afternoon!

To make the day even better, Ethan again wore his favorite socks, Sudsy and Wooly. "They've been good luck to me," he said to Joey when asked about his mismatched socks.

Ethan and his friends welcomed Olivia and listened to her stories about her beloved cat. As the happy kids walked around the corner at Maple Avenue and Main Street, Wooly heard a cat's meow. "Up there, Sudsy," Wooly yelled, pointing at the fur baby's terrible situation.

"Oh, no," Sudsy replied. "That poor kitty is stuck in the tree."

"How can we get the humans to stop walking?" Wooly asked.

"Leave it up to me," Sudsy said with a silly smile. He picked up a bug and placed it on Ethan's leg. The bug crawled slowly up the human's leg and tickled him. Ethan jumped up and down and then danced a few crazy steps!

"What's wrong?" Olivia asked with a half giggle. "Is that a new dance?"

Ethan laughed too. "No. A bug. It was itching my leg. I don't know who put it there."

Sudsy and Wooly laughed.

Ethan picked the bug off his leg and placed it on the ground. "Go away, little bug."

"Look, Ethan, up there," Sudsy said, rolling up and down his leg and pointing toward the big, wide tree.

"Meow," a faint cry reached them.

"Oh, no!" Ethan said. "Look there!"

They watched the cat stare down at them. Then they started to discuss some ideas. "I got it," Olivia said. "I had to solve this problem a few times when my cat would get caught in a tree. I need everyone's help."

"I love ideas, Olivia! What's the plan?" asked Sarah.

"First, we must act quickly. The cat is scared and may try to jump. We have to calm the cat down. Ethan?" She pointed at his feet.

"Yes. I know what to do." He pulled up his pants, making them look like shorts, took Wooly off his foot and rolled him into a ball.

"I'll get a ladder," said Joey.

"We also need to tell an adult," Olivia said. "Safety is important for us too."

"I'll get my Dad," Joey replied.

Joey ran to his house. He came back with his dad and a ladder big enough to reach the cat. Olivia climbed up the ladder with Joey's dad and held out Wooly. "Here kitty, kitty, I'm here to help you," she said. "Do you like our little sock friend? He likes you and wants you to play with him."

"I do?" asked Wooly.

"Yes, you do," yelled Sudsy up to his brother.

"Oh, yes, I do," said Wooly with a forced smile.

Ethan, Sarah, and Joey held onto the ladder.

"Come here, little cutie, come to your little sock friend," said Olivia.

The cat meowed several times and finally pawed at her new sock friend. Wooly laughed as the cat's paws tickled him. Sudsy giggled with the others.

The kitty held onto Wooly and purred while Olivia grabbed the cat. "We got her!" she said.

Ethan, Sarah and Joey cheered as Olivia and Joey's dad came down the ladder with the cat.

"What do we do with the cat now?" asked Joey. "She has no collar or identification."

"We can solve this," Ethan said. "We can put posters up with the cat's picture everywhere."

Sarah lowered her head. "What happens if no one comes to get her?"

"Then the cat will have a new human in me!" Olivia said. "And Seashell will have a sister to play with."

They all smiled.

"What a great day," Ethan said, petting the cat's neck and back.

"I can't wait to do more to help others," Olivia said with a burst of joy.

"And we are a great pair together, too," Sudsy said to Wooly.

"Maybe someday we can again help Ethan and Olivia and their friends," Wooly said.

"When we all are working together, anything is possible," Sudsy said, putting his arm around Wooly.

Michael John Sullivan is the creator of the SockKids. When not looking for his time-traveling SockKids, he is busy writing children's stories and novels. Michael has written several children's sports books for Enslow Publishing. Among the sports figures he has written about are Darryl Strawberry, Barry Bonds, Chris Mullin, Shaquille O'Neal, and Mark Messier.

Michael has also written a novelization based on the popular Digimon animated series, as well as a short story published in *Chicken Soup for the Soul*. His articles have been published by CNN.com, The Huffington Post, The Washington Post, Patch.com and Beliefnet.com.

Shelley Larkin performs many tasks for the SockKids. She develops ideas, co-writes books, and is the marketing and promotions director. She has spent a lifetime of wondering where her missing socks go. The SockKids are grateful to finally solve this mystery for her.

She loves that children and their parents are drawn to the diversity of the SockKids family and the universal and timeless lessons they teach: don't be afraid of new experiences; treat others as you would like to be treated, and of course, beware of the spin cycle! In addition, she is dedicated to finding the right soap for Sudsy.

Alexandra Gold/SugarSnail dreamed of becoming an illustrator since childhood, even though she didn't know the profession actually existed. She later graduated from college with an MFA in graphic design. She never gave up on her dream, so she decided to do what she loved best – become a children's illustrator. Alexandra's/SugarSnail's beautiful artwork can be seen in many children's books. To reach Alexandra Gold/SugarSnail, follow her on Facebook.

The authors would also like to express their gratitude to Debbie Mercer for her skillful editing of this story.

You can find out more about the SockKids at TheSockKids.com.

How to Deal With Bullying: Guidelines for Adults and Children

By Jamie Ross, LMFT
Licensed Marriage and Family Therapist

Bullying can take on many forms and present differently among age groups and across genders. It is most important to first educate your child, friend, or loved one on bullying and be able to identify signs and characteristics of a bully. Bullies are people who have the intention to harm someone emotionally or physically. Most bullies tease or threaten, but sometimes bullies can cause pain, attack, or assert power over another person by physical means.

Signs of bullying often present themselves

through the behaviors of the one we call the "bullied" or the victim. Some signs to look for in a child who is being bullied are avoidant behaviors such as missing school or cutting classes. Some additional signs include isolation from peers or family members and withdrawal from previous interests. Changes in moods and behaviors and drops in self-esteem and confidence could also indicate a bullying situation.

There are different forms of bullying which include cyber bullying, physical aggression, verbal aggression, relational aggression, and sexual harassment. Examples of relational aggression may include spreading rumors or excluding peers in an activity.

Parents, schools, and professionals can take preventative measures when dealing with bullying. Bringing an open awareness to bullying, providing educational information to children and parents, and having supports to promote positive social interactions are just some ways to help children and adults reduce the risk of being bullied.

Some preventative measures include teaching your children how to improve social and interpersonal skills. Parents can help their children by exposing them to social situations where they can practice assertive communication skills and confident approaches to making friends. Children can benefit from exercises that focus on practicing introductions, asking to be a part of an activity, or inviting friends to go out. Focusing on your child's strengths will also help him or her gain the confidence and self-esteem to combat bullying.

Training is important for parents, teachers, and counselors to teach them to observe and detect behavioral changes that would indicate bullying. In addition, it is important to send out anti-bullying messages by modeling a positive, caring, and validating environment and avoiding negative or demeaning attitudes. Creating an environment where feelings are communicated and accepted leads to healthier coping skills. Parents and teachers should set rules and boundaries at home and in classrooms that promote a zero tolerance environment. They should also be on the lookout for children who are likely to be targeted and provide alternative activities for those children who have different interests.

When dealing with cyber bullying, it is important for parents to stay involved in their children's social media networks. Effective parental monitoring such as keeping devices in open areas and sharing passwords to accounts could help to catch and prevent bullying.

When working directly with a child who is actively being bullied, it is important to guide the child to take measures to reduce the harm in the situation. It is a common feeling among parents to believe that interfering in a bullying situation could make the situation intensify. Parents could empower their children to manage the situation appropriately with parental support and at times school and community support. We do know that not taking action at all will continue the bullying.

Some actions that children can take include:

1. Report the incident to an adult you trust.

2. Practice and implement problem-solving skills to diffuse a negative situation (i.e., telling the bully to stop or to leave you alone).
3. Avoid dangerous situations or remove yourself from one.
4. Stay calm and be assertive when communicating.
5. Be a leader.
6. Don't be a bully back.
7. Keep yourself safe. This may include taking a buddy with you to places.
8. Create a safety plan with a parent, teacher, or professional. You can even have a code word with others to indicate when you are feeling threatened.
9. Do not respond to online threats or emails.

Victims should not blame themselves for being bullied and should focus on the characteristics about themselves that make them proud. If you or a friend is experiencing a bullying situation, seek support from a counselor or parent. Some resources to seek additional guidance include your school counselors, local therapists, state department of education, hotlines, and anti-bullying organizations.

Jamie Ross is a New York State Licensed Family and Marriage Therapist working with families, adolescents, individuals and couples to assist clients in exploring possibilities that will facilitate growth, change, and resolution of the relationship problems that are impacting their lives.

Jamie provides treatment for individuals, couples, children, adolescents and families who have a wide variety of relationship, communication, and behavioral issues. Jamie also works with clients who have problems regarding marital and parenting issues. She has extensive experience treating adolescents and their families who have school and social issues, and works extensively with the pre-teen and teen "at risk" population.

As a family therapist, Ross is well-qualified to provide counseling and academic support to students and their families. She is a clinical member of AAMFT (American Association for Marriage and Family Therapy) and is a certified anger management specialist.

What Should I Do If I Get Bullied? (A Quiz)

By Shelley Larkin

Take a moment to look at the questions in this brief quiz. Think about what you know regarding the subject of bullying.

Read the question and circle the letter next to what you believe to be the most appropriate answer. You can check your answers on page 52 but don't look yet!

1. You are walking to school and a gang of older bullies demands your money. Do you:
   a. Fight them?
   b. Shout and run away?
   c. Give them the money?

2. Someone in your class always makes rude comments about you and says them loud enough for you (and others) to hear. It really upsets you. Do you:
   a. Ignore the comments?
   b. Confront the bully and tell him/her off?
   c. Tell the teacher?
   d. Hit the bully?

3. You see someone being bullied. Do you:
   a. Ignore it?
   b. Stop the bully?
   c. Get help?

4. Your former 'best' friends start to bully you. This hurts your feelings and you are quite miserable. Do you:
   a: Tell your parents?
   b. Do nothing?
   c. Call a member of the group to find out why?
   d. Try to find a new group?

5. Some people make racist comments to someone. Do you:
   a. Ignore it and don't get involved?
   b. Get the help of adults to stop the bullies making the comments?
   c. Hit the students making the comments?

6. An adult is bullying you. Do you:
   a. Say nothing?
   b. Tell another adult you trust?
   c. Get some of your friends together and tell the adult to stop?

7. Someone you know is a bully. Do you:
   a. Try to find out why?
   b. Bully him/her?
   c. Try being a friend and setting a good example?

Ten Indicators That Your Child is Being Bullied

By Shelley Larkin

The biggest, most intimidating kid at school with the strongest fists and most aggressive personality is no longer the stereotypical school yard bully. In fact, today's bullies don't just steal lunch money; instead, they ruin reputations and create hurtful rumors using the internet and social media.

However, the negative effects of victimization from a bully are still the same—with kids resorting to depression, social withdrawal, physical injury, addiction, self-harm, and even suicide.

Here are ten possible signs to watch for if you think your child may be the victim of bullying. It's important to note that each indicator listed below should be viewed as a point of reference, not as conclusive evidence of bullying, since other factors may be involved.

1. Unexplained Injuries
2. Changes in Appetite
3. Frequent Sick Days
4. Missing Personal Items
5. Suffering Grades
6. Tendency to Self-Harm
7. Isolation
8. Avoidance
9. Loss of Sleep
10. Exclusion from Social Activities

Shelley Larkin has spent a great deal of time researching the issue of bullying. It is a matter near and dear to her heart as she too was a target and victim of a bully.

See Shelley Larkin's blog post at The SockKids.com discussing her experience with bullying.

Shelley is a passionate child advocate, working with a variety of cause-driven organizations such as Destination Imagination, Up & At It!, Child Abuse Prevention Council, 3 Strands, the International Bullying Prevention Center, and Big Brothers, Big Sisters Youth Organization. Shelley has developed a keen sense of awareness of what children experience today in dealing with such important issues including bullying and recognizes the importance of putting into place the type of value-added programs that will effectively strike a nerve in preventing our youth from losing their way to a safe and productive future.

Answers to: What Should I Do If I Get Bullied?

1. You are walking to school and a gang of older bullies demands your money.
   A: Give them the money; your safety is more important than money. Then make sure to tell an adult you trust what happened.

2. Someone in your class always makes rude comments about you and says them loud enough for you to hear. It really upsets you.
   A: You may feel like punching the bully, but you'll probably be the one to get in trouble if you do. Try ignoring the comments. This is difficult but

the bully might get tired of trying to get a reaction. You should tell your teacher as no one should make hurtful comments to others.

3. You see someone being bullied.
   A: Try to stop it if you can without getting hurt. Let the victim know you're getting help and get a teacher or another adult.

4. Your former "best" friends start to bully you. This hurts your feelings and you are quite miserable.
   A: Try talking to your parents or an adult about this. You can find a new group and make new friends – if these "friends" are so cruel, they may not be worth having as your friends.

5. Some people make racist comments to someone.

   B: Racist comments are wrong and can be very hurtful. Tell an adult about what you heard.

6. An adult is bullying you.

   B: This is a difficult situation for the young person. It would be best to get another adult to help you – someone you trust.

7. Someone you know is a bully.

   C: There are lots of reasons why someone may bully others. If he/she is someone you think you can help, try being a friend to them. The bully may be unhappy and need help from an adult.

How Do You Feel Being Bullied

If you are being bullied, or suspect you might be, you are not alone. Bullying happens to young people everywhere. No matter what, please know that **it's not your fault**. The good news is that you can take steps to protect yourself and others and stop bullying – wherever it is happening.

If you are being bullied, here are some emotions you might be feeling:

Fear ~ Guilt ~ Anger ~ Shame ~ Sadness ~ Pain ~ Despair

If so, don't stifle your feelings. Remember that it is acceptable to cry, punch a pillow, throw rocks into a pond, and capture your feelings on paper.

Tell yourself you can let go of that feeling and help yourself remember that life can be good.

Here is a chance to write about how you feel when you've been bullied. Use a few pieces of paper to write down your thoughts about your experience.